The Empty Hook

By

Joe Dragovich

Illustrated by

Scott Cook

PEYTON & BEN,
THE GIFT OF
CHRISTMAS IS
WITH YOU ☺

Joe Dragovich
11/15/14

nowflake was the new addition to the family Christmas tree. It did not take long for Snowflake to ask the question all new additions to the Christmas tree asked over the last twenty-five years: "Hey, can somebody tell me why there is an empty hook on that branch?"

Pinecone Santa answered, as he had done for the last twenty-five years, "Yes, Snowflake, I can tell you the story of the empty hook."

Snappy, Captain, Hootie, Mr. Chuckles and Abby all smiled as fond memories of Christmases past came rushing back.

"Please do, Pinecone Santa, please do," said an excited Snowflake.

"Please call me Coney Claus. He gave me the name many years ago and we will call you Miss Snowy, if that is okay with you."

ho is he Pinecone – I mean, Coney Claus? Oh, yes, I like Miss Snowy, but who is
he, who is he?" "Slow down, Miss Snowy, slow down. Allow me to introduce you
to some of your new family members. To your right is Gingerbread Boy, he
named him Snappy." Snappy welcomed Miss Snowy with a very warm hello greeting.
"So glad you are here, Miss Snowy. After the story, I will show you around the tree." "Wow, sounds like
fun. I would like that, Snappy. I would like that very much. Thank you." "To your left is Soldier Bear.
He named him Captain." Captain called himself to attention and snapped off a very crisp salute as a greeting to
Miss Snowy. "My, how impressive you are sir. Your uniform is so neat, your boots and buttons so shiny."
"Thank you Miss Snowy, the Captain is always at the ready and at your service." "Hootie the Owl is tucked
away in the branches behind you, Miss Snowy." "My, how cute you are Hootie. I am so pleased to meet you."

With his bright yellow eyes looking over the lenses of his wire framed glasses, Hootie replied with a very scholarly and formal greeting. "The pleasure is all mine my dear Miss Snowy. Welcome to our tree. I am looking forward to visiting with you after the story and throughout this most joyous Christmas season." "He named the Snowman down below you Mr. Chuckles." A puzzled Miss Snowy looked down below and saw Mr. Chuckles the Snowman. Mr. Chuckles looked up and welcomed Miss Snowy to the tree. Sensing Miss Snowy did not understand the name, Mr. Chuckles explained, "I think he thought I was a clown. I have really come to appreciate the name throughout the years." "I think it is a wonderful name, Mr. Chuckles, just wonderful," said Miss Snowy. "Hovering above you is Abigail the Angel. He called her Abby." "Oh my, she is beautiful." "Thank you, Miss Snowy, welcome to our family."

We look forward to Coney Claus telling this story every year. Thank you so much for asking about the empty hook. We hope you enjoy our story as much as we do."

"Well, Miss Snowy, now that we have the introductions out of the way, it is time to tell you our story, the story of The Empty Hook. Our story starts many years ago in a little German village.

"Lauscha, Germany was the home of a very special man. Mr. Mueller was a gifted German glassblower. His family's history in the art of glassblowing can be traced back to the 1500s.

"His family made its way to Lauscha, Germany in the 1700s. He was a ninth generation glassblower. Mr. Mueller made drinking glasses, bowls, plates and vases. His work was very good and he enjoyed seeing the reactions of his customers when they picked up their orders.

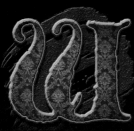hen the days grew shorter and the air colder, Mr. Mueller began making Christmas ornaments. His ornaments were extraordinary and his customers were dazzled by them. His customers were often speechless when they picked up their orders. Mr. Mueller included a small card with each order of ornaments. The card was a reminder, a message Mr. Mueller shared with his customers: 'The gift of Christmas is with you, remember Him on His day.'

"Mr. Mueller poured his heart and soul into his craft. It was his way of celebrating the true meaning of Christmas. He never forgot the story of the first Christmas. He remembered the magic of that special night in Bethlehem and the greatest gift ever given to all of mankind.

"He would smile and feel gratified when his customers invited him into their homes to see how beautiful and magical their Christmas trees looked when decorated with his glass ornaments. The red, green, blue, silver and gold glass balls, along with candy, animals, fruit and holiday characters, were breathtaking. Mr. Mueller was most pleased when his customers greeted him with his message: 'The gift of Christmas is with you, remember Him on His day.'

The village Burgermeister was so impressed with Mr. Mueller's spectacular glass ornaments, he enlisted Mr. Mueller to make ornaments to decorate the village Christmas tree. The Burgermeister said, 'Mr. Mueller, the gift of Christmas is certainly within you. Please share your gift with our village.'

M r. Mueller was very pleased. He made even more spectacular ornaments and the village Christmas tree became another way for Mr. Mueller to celebrate the true meaning of Christmas. He made a special set of glass balls and wrote his message on them for all to see: 'The gift of Christmas is with you, remember Him on His day.'

The gift of Christmas is with you

Remember Him on his day

A nobleman from a far away village heard of Mr. Mueller's Christmas ornaments and traveled to Lauscha to hire him. The nobleman needed a special set of ornaments for his young son, Milo, who was ill. The nobleman shared Mr. Mueller's appreciation for the true meaning of Christmas. He, too, remembered the story of that special night in Bethlehem.

"The nobleman placed his order for several glass balls of all colors. The nobleman ordered a special set of characters: Pinecone Santa, Gingerbread Boy, Soldier Bear, Owl, Snowman, Angel and Elf. The nobleman explained these were some of his son's favorites, especially Elf.

r. Mueller created his most spectacular set of ornaments ever for the nobleman's son. Mr. Mueller used the finest sand and heated it to perfection. Mr. Mueller blew each piece while the message, 'The gift of Christmas is with you, remember Him on His day,' played over and over in his mind.

The nobleman traveled back to his village, arriving on Christmas Eve, only to find Milo's illness had worsened. The nobleman was devastated. He opened the ornaments and read the card to Milo: 'The gift of Christmas is with you, remember Him on His day.'

"Milo smiled a wide smile and his eyes reflected the images of Pinecone Santa, Gingerbread Boy, Soldier Bear, Owl, Snowman, Angel and Elf. Milo's health improved and on Christmas morning, he was able to place his special set of ornaments on the Christmas tree for the first time.

"The family celebrated Christmas and recited Mr. Mueller's message to each other and shouted it to everybody they met on that Christmas Day: 'The gift of Christmas is with you, remember Him on His day.'

uring the days that followed, young Milo gave each of the ornaments a name with one exception. Elf remained Elf. Milo adored Elf from the moment he saw him. He would sneak Elf off the Christmas tree and into his room from time to time throughout the years. One year he took Elf to school with him. He even managed to keep Elf out of storage for an entire year.

"Elf had quite an adventure during that year. He went fishing and hiking. He was chased by a dog and fell off of a wagon. He actually was with Milo and his father when they cut down our Christmas tree that year. Elf said Milo's father was so surprised to see him on the tree moments after the tree was placed in the stand.

hose were wonderful magical times we all shared with Milo," said Abby. "The bond between Elf and Milo was so strong and so beautiful. We knew Milo cared greatly for all of us, but Elf was special. It was difficult to watch Milo grow up. As young boys become young men, they take on more responsibility and their interests change.

he season became even more special for all of us, as it was the only time we would spend with Milo. Each year, when Milo would open our box, it was as if he was eight years old again. He would smile a wide smile and greet us with a loving hand. We were always so excited and eager to see where he would place us on the Christmas tree. Milo always seemed to find just the right spot for each of us.

"The years passed by and Milo was once again in poor health, but Milo was now an old man. It was Christmas Eve and eighty-three years to the day since Milo first saw us. He was now ninety-one years old.

ilo looked upon his special set of ornaments and knew it would be the last time. He bravely smiled a wide smile. His eyes twinkled, but his hand trembled as he placed each ornament on the family Christmas tree one last time. His family watched and listened as he placed Coney Claus, Snappy, Captain, Hootie, Mr. Chuckles, Abby and Elf on the family Christmas tree. After each ornament was hung, he would say, 'The gift of Christmas is with you, remember Him on His day.'

T he family noticed that Milo placed Elf on the Christmas tree last this time. For the last eighty-three years, Elf was always hung first and put away last. As a young boy, Milo would say, 'Elf gets the pick of the tree, so he goes first.' When it was time to take the Christmas tree down, he would say, 'Elf goes last so I can keep him out the longest.'

On Christmas morning, Milo was too weak to get out of bed. His family gathered around and comforted him. They celebrated Christmas and shared stories from Christmases past. In the early morning hours on the day after Christmas, the family was awakened by the sound of shattering glass. Elf was in pieces on the floor. His hook was still hung on the branch where Milo had placed him on Christmas Eve. The family went to Milo's room. Milo was at peace. His hands held Mr. Mueller's card. 'The gift of Christmas is with you, remember Him on His day.'

The following year on Christmas Eve, and every year after, the family would place an empty hook on the Christmas tree after all the ornaments were hung. They remembered Milo and his special set of ornaments. They would share Mr. Mueller's message, remembering the story of the first Christmas and then they celebrated the gift of Christmas."

"Miss Snowy, now you know the story of The Empty Hook," said Coney Claus.

Miss Snowy replied, "The hook really isn't empty, Elf is still there, isn't he?"

"Yes he is, Miss Snowy, yes he is, and so is our young Milo. The gift of Christmas is with you, remember Him on His day."

Snappy, Captain, Hootie, Mr. Chuckles and Abby all smiled.

Cover and interior artwork by Scott Cook.

WestBow Press books may be ordered through booksellers or by contacting:

WestBow Press
A Division of Thomas Nelson
1663 Liberty Drive
Bloomington, IN 47403
www.westbowpress.com
1-(866) 928-1240

ISBN: 978-1-4497-7819-4 (sc)
ISBN: 978-1-4497-7820-0 (e)

Library of Congress Control Number: 2012922789

Printed in the United States of America by Bookmasters
Ashland OH
July 2013
M11074

WestBow Press rev. date: 06/27/2013

WestBow
PRESS
A DIVISION OF THOMAS NELSON